In a tank by the window, so sparkly and bright,
lived Gill Bill the fish, swimming day and night.
His fins shimmered colors, a dazzling array,
a happy little fish in his watery play.

One day while swimming, something caught his eye,
a pebble that glowed like stars in the sky.
It shimmered and sparkled with a magical gleam,
Gill Bill thought, "Could this be part of a dream?"

He swam round the pebble, curiosity high,
the water swirled fast as he floated by.
With a gentle nudge, the magic began,
and suddenly, Gill Bill flew over the land!

Out of his tank and into the air,
Gill Bill was flying without a care!
The world was so big, full of sights to see,
Gill Bill was soaring, happy and free.

He flew past the flowers, the trees so tall;
the birds sang songs, giving him a call.
Butterflies danced as he floated near,
Gill Bill waved with a fin, full of cheer.

He glided and spun, light as a cloud,
soaring and twirling, feeling so proud.
But soon his belly began to ache,
it was time for a snack—no room for mistake!

He floated to the kitchen, and what did he see?
Three tasty meatballs, waiting for me!
He gobbled them up, one, two, three,
"They'll give me strength to fly so free!"

With his tummy full, he flew once more,
exploring the world, ready to soar.
The wind was gentle; the sky so wide,
Gill Bill wiggled his fins, enjoying the ride.

Up in the sky, soaring so high,
Gill Bill spotted a bird flying by.
"Hello there, fish! What brings you here?"
Chirped the bird with a song full of cheer.

"I found a pebble with magical light;
it lifted me up to join your flight!"
The bird flapped her wings, circling around,
"A fish in the sky? That's quite profound!"

With a joyful trill, the bird flew near,
"Enjoy your flight, there's nothing to fear!"
Gill Bill waved with a gleam in his eye,
as they both danced together in the sky.

Through the trees, he soared with ease,
when a squirrel appeared between the leaves.
"Hello there, fish! What brings you near?"
Chattered the squirrel with a twitch of cheer.

"I've found a pebble that made me fly,
lifting me up to the bright blue sky!"
The squirrel blinked, tail twitching with glee,
"A flying fish? How can that be?"

With a laugh, the squirrel gave a flip,
"Enjoy your flight—what a magical trip!"
Gill Bill waved as he floated away,
off to explore the rest of the day.

Fur & Feathers, What Do We Have In Common

A Story of Appreciating Our Differences And Finding Our Similarities

Ellen K. Fischer

United States Copyright Registration Number TXu2-292-219

Website: www.ellenkfischer.com

Illustrator: Avery Tiegs

DEDICATION

I would like to dedicate this book to my husband Mike. My biggest cheerleader and supporter and the best dad and Papa our five daughters and grandkids could ask for.

ACKNOWLEDGMENT

I could not have taken this journey without the unwavering support of my husband, Michael.

ABOUT THE AUTHOR

Ellen Fischer is the mom of five grown daughters and two grandchildren. She grew up in a small city in southeastern Wisconsin and resides with her husband not far from where she grew up. Ellen has always loved writing and is an avid reader. She has a bachelor's degree in Management and Communication and an MBA in Management. Ellen's dream is to write more children's books that help children and adults to navigate our world by leading with kindness, compassion, and strength.

PREFACE

I wrote this book because I feel it's important to send the message to our children that there is nothing wrong with being different and unique. We live in a wonderful, beautiful, and diverse world. Every time I watch the birds at my feeders, I think about each bird's unique beauty and yet, they are so similar. My message is that we need to embrace our differences and celebrate the ways we are similar.

The backyard was busier than normal with activity. It was getting close to winter.

The squirrels were busy gathering food, digging up the seeds they had hidden over the summer, and making their nests cozier for the long winter ahead.

The birds were eating seeds and the last of the berries, and adding sticks to their nests.

The families in the neighborhood were also busy getting ready for winter. They were raking leaves, preparing their gardens for the winter, and making sure they had warm boots, coats, and hats.

Mr. Owl observed all these activities from high in his tree and began to wonder why the animals couldn't help each other prepare for the winter. For he was a wise, old owl who watched many winters come and go.

Every autumn the animals prepared for winter, but they got ready for the long winter alone.

Mr. Owl had an idea. He was going to talk to the animals in the backyard about their preparations for winter. He decided to talk to the birds and the squirrels first as they seemed to scurry and fly around the most getting ready for winter.

at would they listen? Squirrels have fur and birds have feathers. They seemed so different from each other.

Mr. Owl wondered if they would see what they have in common. He was filled with hope that he could get the birds and the squirrels to see what they had in common, and learn to appreciate how they were wonderfully unique.

He had also seen how the birds were masters of flying and cracking open seeds with their beaks.

Mr. Owl delivered the invitations to the birds and the squirrels for a backyard meeting to talk about getting ready for winter. He hoped the birds and squirrels would come to the meeting.

Being a wise owl, he knew cooperation worked the best and made hard work easier. He had seen it many times with the people who lived in the neighborhood.

He had seen Mr. Chadwick and his children help Mrs. Joseph rake her leaves, because she lives alone.

Mr. Owl was excited and nervous the day of the meeting, because he knew the birds and squirrels may only see their differences and not what makes them similar.

The day of the meeting was here! Mr. Owl had snacks prepared. Seeds and freshwater because the birds and squirrels love both.

Mr. Owl sat on the stump of a tree and watched as the squirrels and the birds started arriving for the meeting. He noticed that the birds and the squirrels didn't sit together and he wondered why.

Mr. Owl asked the birds and the squirrels why they did not sit together. The birds said, "We have feathers, not fur, and we fly, we don't scurry along the ground and run up trees. What could we have in common with the squirrels?"

The squirrels said that they have fur and not feathers and they run and scurry up trees. What could they have in common with the birds?

Mr. Owl realized that convincing the birds and the squirrels to help each other was going to be a challenge, but one he knew, would help the birds and the squirrels over the long cold winter.

Mr. Owl asked the birds and the squirrels what their favorite food was, and at the same time they all said seeds. The birds and the squirrels looked at each other and smiled.

Mr. Owl asked another question. "Is water important to you and your family?" A loud "yes" from the birds and the squirrels. This time they all laughed.

Mr. Owl asked one more question. "Is it important that you have a warm secure nest for the winter?" The birds and the squirrels got very quiet, they looked at each other and once again, they smiled.

Mr. Owl smiled as he watched the birds and the squirrels talk about how they could help each other get ready for winter. You see, they had seen their differences, and had also realized what makes them the same.

After that meeting the birds and squirrels met every week to help each other, gather food and prepare their nests for the long winter ahead.

On the first night of winter, Mr. Owl told his family that while birds have feathers and fly, and squirrels have fur and run, that they came to appreciate what makes them unique, to accept their differences, and focus on how they can help each other.

Discussion Guide - How to apply the lessons from Fur and Feathers

The purpose of this discussion guide is to help children and the reader understand how to apply the lessons from this book to their lives.

- Appreciating our differences
    - o Ask if they like salads and note the different ingredients and how when they are mixed together they make a delicious salad.
- Celebrating what makes us wonderfully unique
    - o Highlight how a band or orchestra is made up of many different instruments but create a beautiful melody.
- Finding similarities and ways we can help each other to unite.
    - o Ask the children to look around at their friends and point out what makes them unique.
    - o Ask the children how many like pizza or cookies and then point out what their similarities are.
    - o Discuss how we can help out our friends or neighbors.

Made in the USA
Monee, IL
05 January 2025

Through the woods, he drifted slow,
when a raccoon peeked from down below.
"Hello there, fish! How'd you get here?"
Asked the raccoon with a curious cheer.

"I found a pebble, magic and bright,
it lifted me up and gave me flight!"
The raccoon scratched his head with a grin,
"A flying fish? Well, that's a win!"

With a wink, the raccoon gave a playful nod,
"Enjoy your travels, what an odd!"
Gill Bill smiled and waved goodbye,
as he floated onward through the sky.

Down to the pond, he floated with grace,
where a frog sat with a big, wide face.
"Hello there, fish! How'd you get here?"
Asked the frog with a friendly cheer.

"I found a pebble that's magic," Bill said,
"It lifted me up from where I once lay!"
The frog grinned wide and gave a small nod,
"Enjoy your flight, little fish—how odd!"

His adventure continued through the day.
Gill Bill waved as he floated away,
the sky turned pink, the sun sinking low,
but he wasn't ready to let go.

The stars came out, twinkling bright,
Gill Bill soared in the soft moonlight.
But soon he yawned; feeling sleepy inside,
it was time to rest from his magical ride.

Through the window he flew, into his space,
the water felt soft, a cool embrace.
He swam in circles, his heart full of light,
his cozy tank felt just right.

The magic pebble now faded away,
its glow disappearing at the end of the day.
Gill Bill snuggled in his little cave,
thinking of all the fun he'd crave.

And so ends the tale of Gill Bill's flight,
a magical journey through day and night.
He soared with joy, but learned it's true;
home is the place where dreams come through!

The End

Made in the USA
Monee, IL
05 January 2025